Expressway Jewels

고속도로의 보석들

Story by Evangeline Nicholas

Illustrations by Victor Bougaev

"Oh, this is all wrong!
It's just not working!"
moaned my sister, Yung Lim.
She was working on a dress
to wear on dress-up day
at the high school.

My mother had given her
a piece of rich blue silk.
But now Yung Lim
was having trouble
coming up with a pattern
for the beading.

옷을 입습니다.

3

After dinner I asked my sister
if she could take me up
to the sixteenth floor of our
building. I wanted to look out
the windows of the community
room to see the lights of the city.

As we rode the elevator, I was
wishing that I had an important
project like Yung Lim's.
When she was finished,
everyone would compliment
her on her beautiful beadwork.
They would say that she is
an honor to our family.

우리는 16층에 가기 위해
엘리베이터를 탔습니다.

4

But when the elevator doors
opened, I put my thoughts
behind me and ran over
to look out the windows.
I could see for miles and miles.

The lights on the expressway
were tiny but very bright.

All the colors looked
so beautiful together.

우리는 창문 밖을 보았습니다.

"The green lights look like
sour balls," I said.

But Yung Lim said,
"They look like emeralds
to me. That's Mom's
birthstone."

"The yellow lights look like
lemon drops," I said.

But Yung Lim said,
"They are like yellow
citrine gems."

신 사탕,

에메랄드,

레몬즙

8

"When I look at all of the lights together, I think of a ton of delicious jelly beans," I said.

Yung Lim laughed.

"I think the red lights look like red hot candies," I said.

But Yung Lim said,
"They look like rubies to me."
Yung Lim loves rubies.

"The white lights look like diamonds," said Yung Lim.

10

루비, 다이아몬드, 보석사탕

11

"No matter what you think
they look like, Yung Lim, I love
all the colors of the lights and
the patterns they make," I said.

나는 모든 색깔을 좋아합니다.

"That's it!" Yung Lim exclaimed.
"Look at the lights!
And all the colors!
They make a beautiful pattern.
That's my pattern for the beadwork!"

She gave me a big hug.
"Thanks, Yung Soo."

I felt so proud!

14

누나는 나를 껴안았습니다.

15